WHERE THE CAT LED...

by

Hazel Stuart

illustrated by

Georgie Beable

Grosvenor House
Publishing Limited

The right of Hazel Stuart to be identified as the author of this
work has been asserted in accordance with Section 78
of the Copyright, Designs and Patents Act 1988

Illustrated by Georgie Beable

This book is published by
Grosvenor House Publishing Ltd
Link House
140 The Broadway, Tolworth, Surrey, KT6 7HT.
www.grosvenorhousepublishing.co.uk

A CIP record for this book
is available from the British Library

ISBN 978-1-83975-011-3

Dedication

"For Isabella".

For as long as she could remember, Isabella had gone to stay at Watermouth Castle in the summer holidays with her family. This year, with the others all grown up, her mum invited her auntie and her cousin along for company.

On the first morning, she woke up to find there was no one in the apartment. She looked all around but Mum was not in the kitchen or on the bench outside - and Auntie Alison and James were nowhere to be seen either.

All the beds had been made and the dishes had been done, so she could tell they'd had breakfast already. The sun was shining in through the open door and she looked across the courtyard but couldn't see them anywhere.

She was just beginning to worry that they'd forgotten all about her, when she noticed a piece of paper propped up on the table.

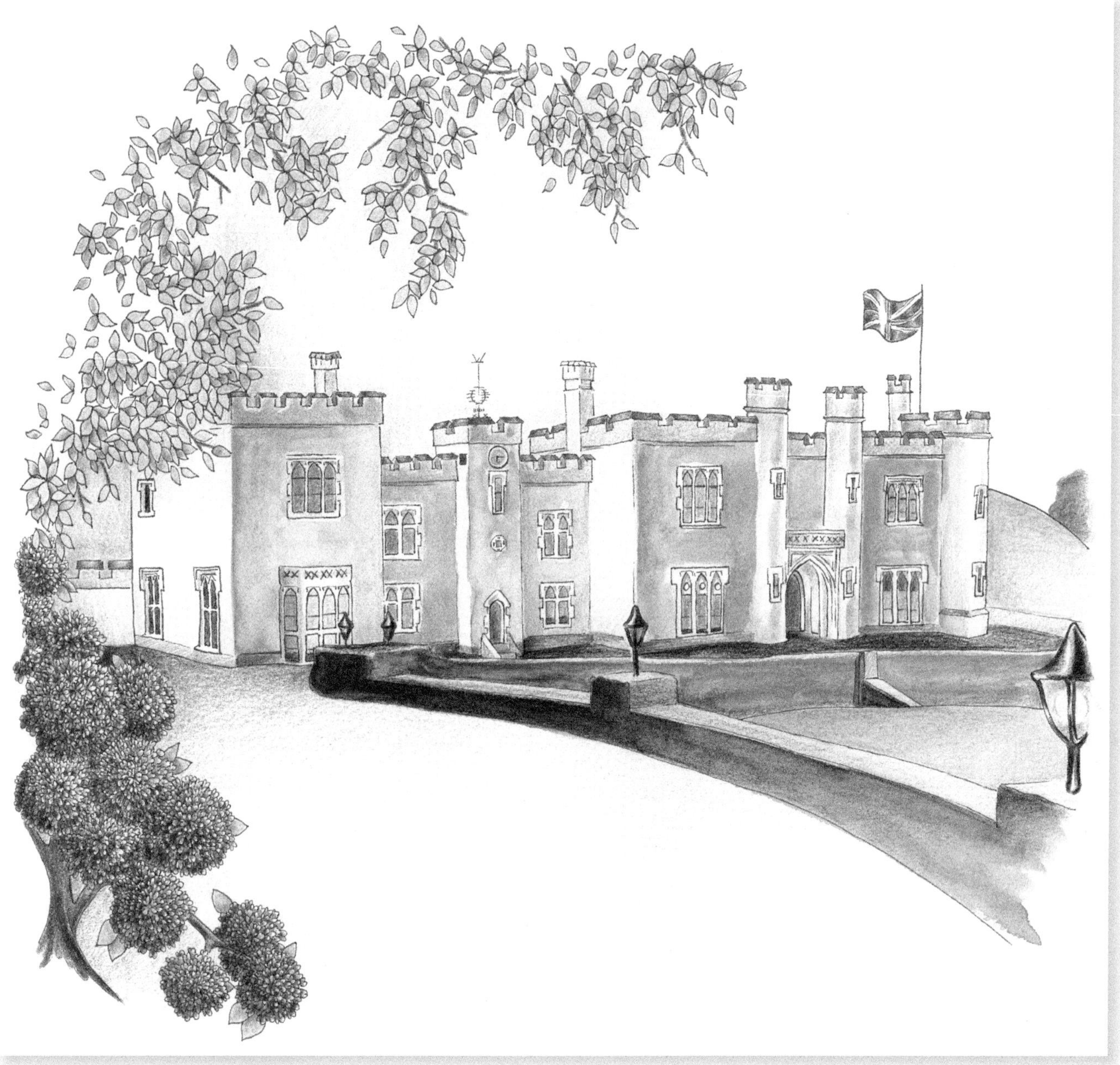

It was a note in her mum's handwriting. They'd all gone for a swim.

It was the first time she'd been left alone - but they weren't far away, just across the courtyard.

'And anyway, I *am* nine now,' she thought, feeling quite grown up.

She looked around. What should she do? Join the others and go swimming?

All she really wanted to do today was go and explore the park. She couldn't wait to go to Gnomeland again… and Adventure Land… and Merry-Go-Land with all the rides!

She'd been saving up 2ps and 10ps all year for the slot machines and yesterday, on the long car journey, she'd made a secret pact with herself that she'd be brave this time and even go into the terrifying 'Smugglers' Dungeon' in the museum…

…but it was Gnomeland that she wanted to go to first. It was always the best.

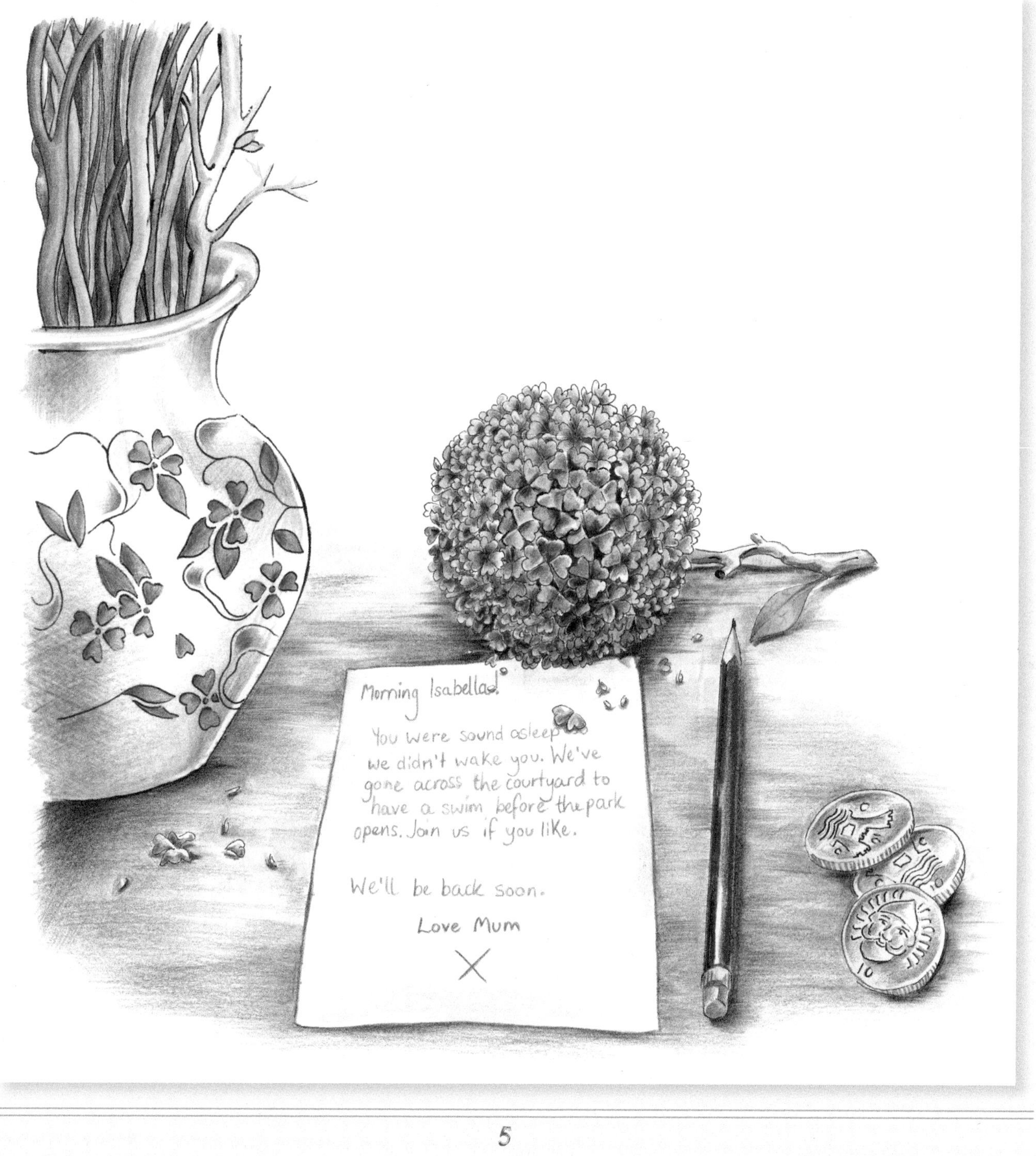
Morning Isabella!
You were sound asleep so
we didn't wake you. We've
gone across the courtyard to
have a swim before the park
opens. Join us if you like.
We'll be back soon.
Love Mum
X

You could pan for gold and have it made into Gnome money – or 'gnold' as they called it - and there were caves to go in and steps that made noises as you stepped on them. Best of all though, you could explore the gnome village and peek in the windows, spying on what the little people were doing at home. She knew they were only models with clockwork inside and not really alive, but it didn't matter a bit. She loved it.

Isabella decided to get dressed so that she would be ready as soon as the others came back. She had unpacked her suitcase the night before, putting all her clothes neatly in the lovely big chest of drawers in her room. That way she could pretend she lived in the castle all the time, like a princess.

She opened the top drawer. One pair of pants.

Did she need socks? Probably not.

She had nice white sandals to wear that Mum had bought her especially for the holidays. She didn't need socks with them.

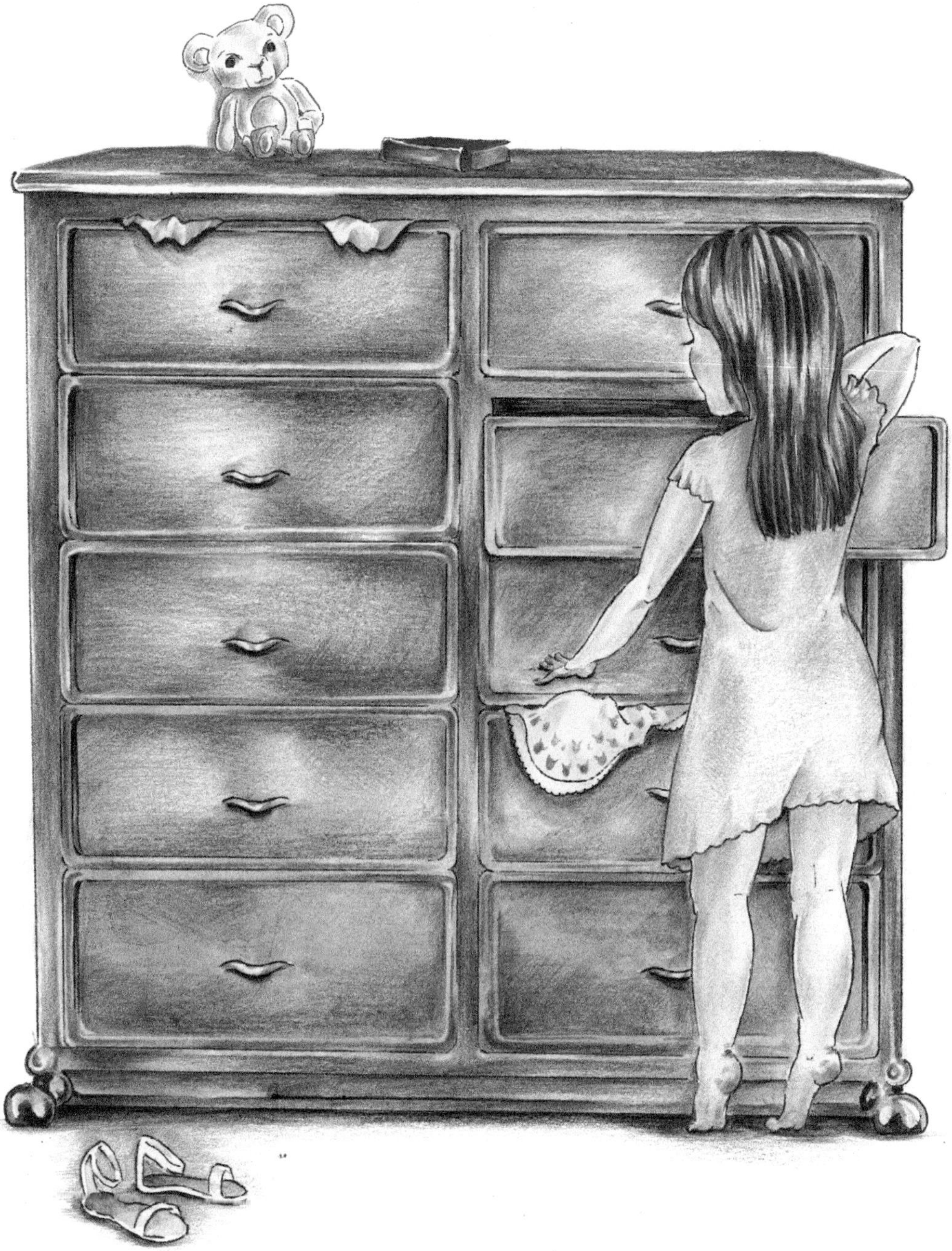

Throwing the pants on the bed, she closed the top drawer and opened another below.

'Ah yes! My cat dress!'

She loved cats and this was her favourite dress because it had cats all over it.

She pulled it out of the drawer, excited to wear it. What a good day it was going to be! The first day at Watermouth Castle and she had her favourite dress to wear!

She put her clothes on quickly, wanting to be ready as soon as the others came in. However, even after she had fastened the buckles on her sandals, had brushed her hair and had been ready and waiting for some time, there was no sign of them returning soon.

Isabella sighed. They were going to take such a long time.

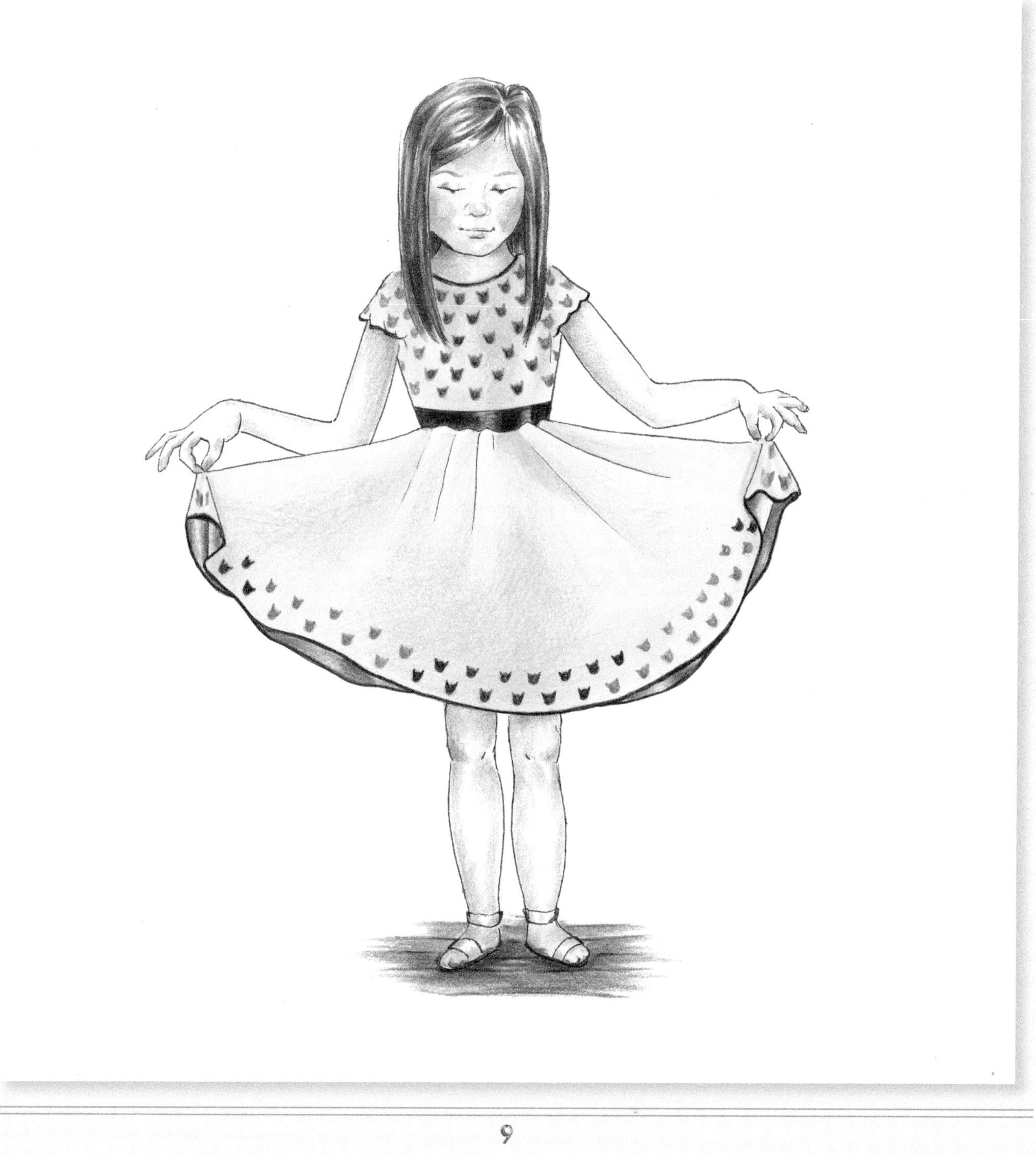

Just then, she caught sight of the castle cat, a large ginger and white puss, who she had made friends with in years gone by. She stepped out the door and crouched down.

"Puss. Puss. Come here, Puss," she said softly, rubbing her thumb and fingers together to attract its attention.

The cat stopped in its tracks and licked its paw. It glanced at her, as if it wasn't sure who she was talking to.

"Come on, Puss," she said again reassuringly.

The ginger cat looked at her and began cautiously to walk towards her.

"You remember me, don't you? I'm Isabella. I came last year. You've still to tell me your name."

She stroked the thick fur around its neck and under its chin, which all cats seem to love. The ginger castle cat purred loudly and circled around and around her bended knees, until finally it moved off in the direction of the park.

"Oh, goodbye then Puss," Isabella said sadly.

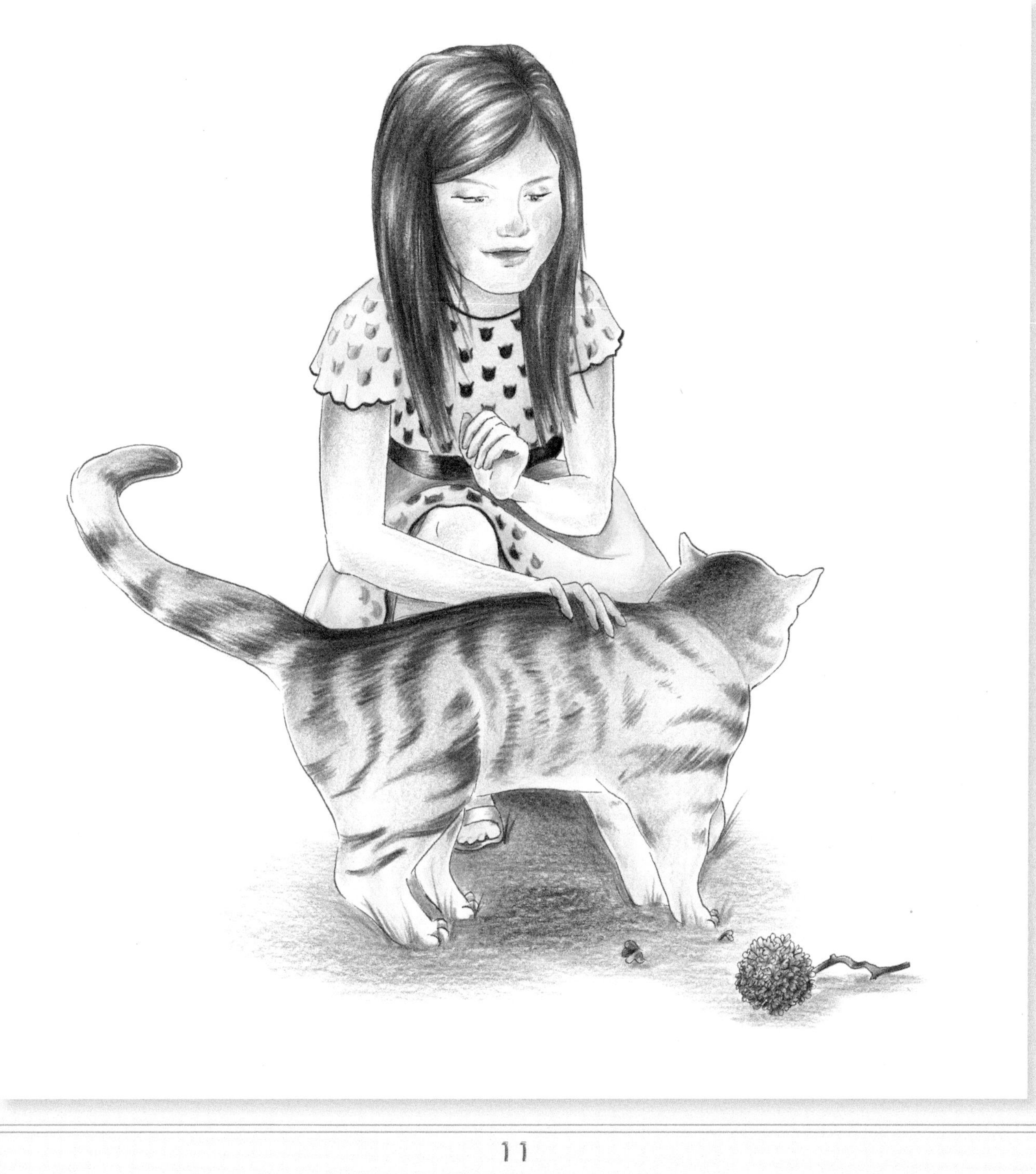

Just then the cat stopped abruptly and looked at her, as if it was trying to tell her something.

"What's up Puss?"

The cat came back, circled her legs again and then made for the park gate, stopping and looking round at her just as before.

"Have you got something to show me?" Isabella asked.

Clearly it wanted her to follow it. She knew she ought to wait for the others but it wouldn't hurt to go a little way.

If you were staying in the castle, you were allowed to go up into the park whenever you liked. It was quite safe. The rides weren't on and the café was shut but you could still walk around and look at everything. She'd done it with Mum loads of times. It wasn't like she could get lost; she knew her way around.

She decided she'd just go and see what the cat wanted to show her and be back before the others had finished their swim. She wouldn't be long and they'd probably never notice.

Just in case, Isabella popped back indoors, found her favourite pen on the dresser and, turning Mum's note over, she wrote a note of her own on the other side.

"Gone for a walk in the park with the cat. Be back soon.
Isabella. x"

Then she stepped out the door. The ginger puss was waiting for her and seemed quite impatient now. She followed it across the courtyard and round to the gate.

As she passed the pool house, she peeked in and saw James squealing with laughter in the water. He looked like he was having great fun.

The cat jumped up on to the gate ahead and back down on the other side. It was a big gate and it looked heavy but it swung open easily when Isabella undid the latch and it was not too difficult to close behind her.

Ahead was the woodland walkway, dark beneath the trees. Her friendly guide jumped onto the wall and made its way between the grassy roots and toadstools. Isabella skipped along the familiar path, so intent on keeping track of the ginger fur amongst the undergrowth that she did not even stop to look at the amusements along the way.

Soon enough they came to a fork in the path, left for Gnomeland and right for the rest of the park. By this time, the cat was quite out of reach, treading its own path through the woods and the craggy rocks towards the gnome village high above.

Isabella skipped round to the left and was distracted for a moment by the happy little gnome, up high on the cliff, greeting everyone.

"Welcome to Gnomeland!" he called.

"Hello," she replied, smiling shyly.

She wasn't sure if he could hear her - he was only a puppet after all - but somewhere in the back of her mind she remembered it was rude to ignore a gnome if they spoke to you and it could bring you bad luck.

When she turned around, the cat had disappeared entirely. She looked up and down the path disappointedly but it was nowhere to be seen.

Thinking she'd catch up with it eventually, she carried on and entered into the first of the caves. It was dark inside but she pressed the big white button and instantly the place came to life.

Isabella peered through the glass windows on either side of the tunnel, watching the underground gnomes, who were hard at work. With their pickaxes and digging machines, they were unearthing sparkling gems from the rocks: rubies and diamonds and glittering emeralds.

She blinked as she came out the other side of the cave. It seemed brighter and sunnier outside than it had before. Then something seemed to move out of the corner of her eye. It was too big to be the cat. Was it another child?

Whoever it was had disappeared around a bend. Isabella quickened her steps, hoping she'd catch up with them. They must be staying in the castle too. A holiday friend. She would introduce them to James and they could all play together.

Excited at the thought, she carried on up the path, which took her further and further into the gnomes' hillside village.

She had always loved the sweet log cabins that the gnomes called home, with their checked curtains and the pretty cut-out hearts on their shutters and doors. When she had been younger, maybe six or seven, she could have walked inside quite easily, without ducking at all – if the doors hadn't all been locked.

They were just displays really and the gnomes were just puppets, but it all felt so real - and real or not, it was so much fun to run from one little house to the other, peering in the windows and pressing the buttons to make the scenes come to life.

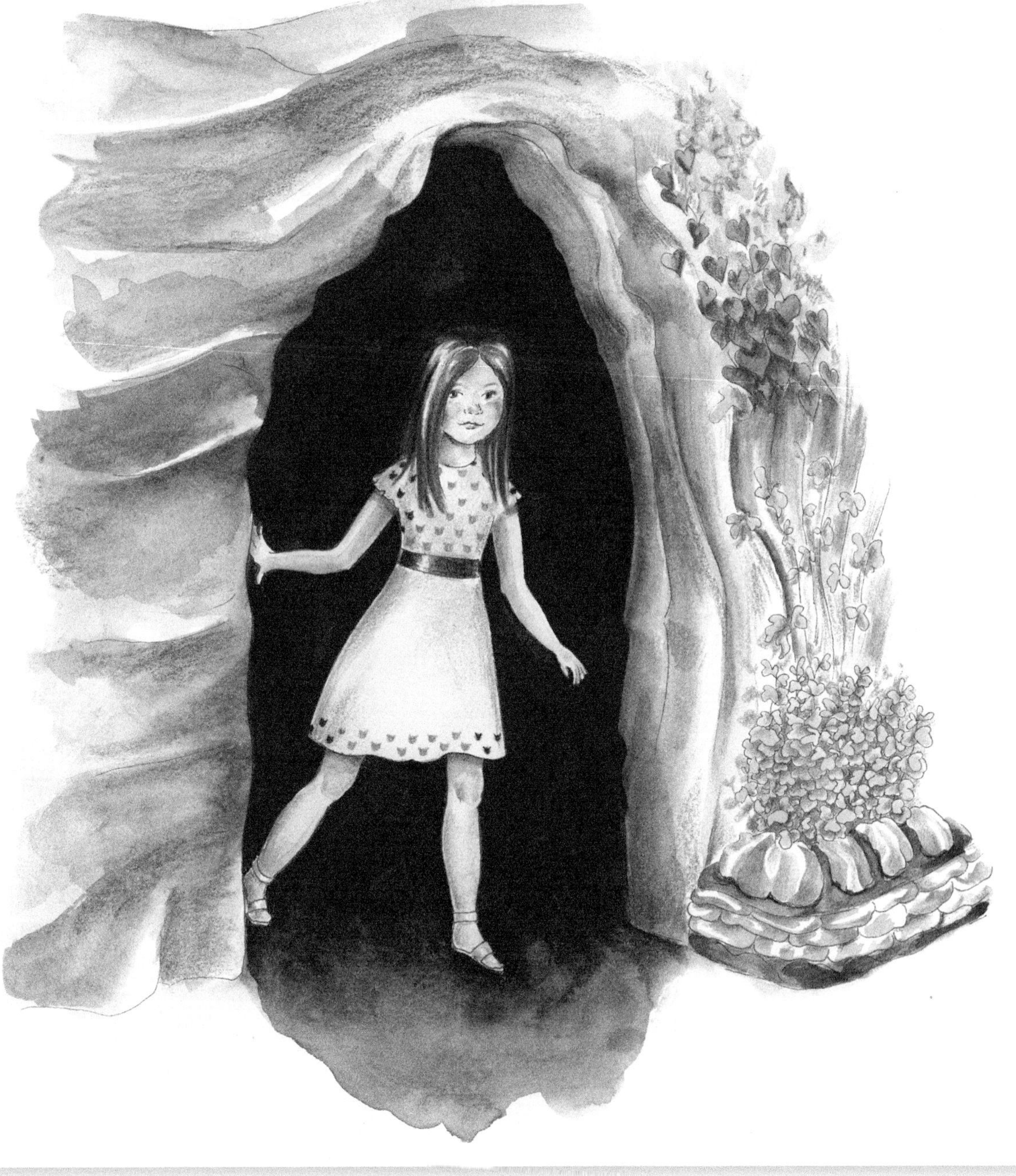

Now she realised that there was no sign of the cat or the child anymore and she began to slow down.

'Perhaps my eyes were playing tricks on me,' she thought.

Everything was still. The only sounds she could hear were the birds chit-chatting to themselves in the bushes and the trees around her.

To her right, in one small cabin, was a gnome family having their afternoon tea. She peeked through the glass and pressed the button on the wall. Just as in the cave, the light came on, the music started and the gnomes came to life - these ones lifting their merry little teacups instead of pickaxes. Isabella laughed. Everything was just as she remembered it.

However the cakes on the tiny table made her feel hungry all of a sudden. Why had she not thought to have some breakfast before she left?

"Oh well," she said to herself, as the music finished and the light in the gnome's house cut off. "I'll just walk through the village then go back."

She climbed the stairs at the side of the little house. They were wooden ones that hugged the wall of the cabin and led up to the gold-panning area and the path beyond.

They looked like ordinary steps but Isabella knew from before that they were enchanted.

"Ooh."

"Eek."

"Ay up!"

"Ouch!"

They called out to her, one after the other, as she stepped on them.

Being older now, she knew they weren't really enchanted and assumed each step was linked to a speaker, but she'd believed they were truly magical when she'd been small and it was nice to believe it still…

"Well, hello there young lady," said a gruff voice ahead, startling her.

Isabella froze. Who was this? Had she been caught? Was she in trouble?

There, standing at the top of the wooden steps, and eye to eye with her now that she was more than half way up, was a little man. He had a wispy, pointed beard and rosy cheeks, and looked just like a gnome - but he couldn't be, for he was clearly alive!

"Hello," she said uncertainly, her eyes wide with wonder.

He didn't reply and just stared at her with a frown.

"I'm Isabella," she said, the words tumbling out her mouth. "I'm staying in the castle with my family. We come here every year…"

She realised she was nervous. Everyone knows you are not supposed to talk to strangers. Somewhere though, deep in her heart, she felt sure this was a real gnome and she did not want any bad luck at the start of her holiday.

The little man stroked his beard and his face relaxed into a smile.

"I think I remember you, Isabella. You were here last time when the hydrangeas were in flower."

She wasn't sure which flowers he meant, but she nodded and smiled, glad that he didn't seem angry with her anymore.

"I'm sorry," she said, "I'll go back now. I'm hungry anyway…"

She began to turn away, lowering her foot onto the step below.

"Ouch!" the step cried out.

"Those silly steps! Don't they realise that's what they were built for?" said the gnome, laughing.

Isabella laughed too. It was so true. How could a step complain about being stood on?

"You say you are hungry? Would you like to have breakfast with us?" asked the little man.

Isabella looked at him. Her tummy was rumbling now.

"Really? Why, yes! Although I mustn't be long or my mum will worry."

The little man was delighted. He hopped and skipped and clapped his hands.

"I do hope you like porridge," he said. "My name is Gaffey. Come and meet my wife. She'll be so pleased to have a nice girl like you join us."

Isabella followed along behind him, as they went even further up the path, wondering if she was in a dream. He was so tiny but his short legs seemed very strong, for he had no trouble getting up the hill. She watched the point of his hat as it swung to and fro in front of her, realising that she was quite a bit taller than him.

Presently they came to a log cabin whose door faced up the hill. There was no window to the left nor to the right of the entrance. It had a little semi-circular, gravel garden, crossed by a paved path that led to the door.

She didn't remember this from before. Surely it must have been here last year though as it fitted right in and it didn't look new.

The doorway was a little short for Isabella - now that she was nine - but when Gaffey opened it, she was determined that she was not going to miss this chance to go into a gnome house for anything! She ducked her head and followed him through.

Inside, the room was filled with a lovely smell and, side by side, were two high chairs, each with a baby gnome in it. They were gurgling happily together and Isabella thought they were very cute.

"Hey Glenda!" Gaffey said to his wife. "I found this girl down by the silly steps."

The lady gnome, who had a shiny, happy face that was really very pretty, came forward, beaming, and clasped Isabella by the hands.

"How lovely!" she said. "You will stay for breakfast? I have made much too much porridge as usual."

Isabella was given a chair to sit in. It was a small chair - of course, being made for a gnome - but she fitted on it comfortably. The babies, who were next to her, grinned at her in delight. They were so sweet Isabella smiled back and soon she was playing and laughing with them.

"That's Nona and this is Noggin," Glenda said.

Nona and Noggin. Gaffey and Glenda. Gnomes certainly had funny names.

Gaffey passed the porridge around. Isabella wasn't sure she liked porridge but she was so hungry she decided to try it.

"Ooh! This is lovely!" she exclaimed – and truly it was.

When she had eaten it all, she played with the twins some more. Glenda made two warm bottles of milk, one for each of the babies, and Isabella asked if she could help feed one.

"Why, my dear, you are such a helpful girl!" Glenda said, handing her a bottle. "It is so difficult to feed two babies at once. Gaffey and I do it together when we can but often he's got to go down into the mines and I have to do it all by myself."

Isabella enjoyed helping Glenda. She fed little Nona, who gazed lovingly up into her eyes as she drank, whilst Gaffey fed Noggin. Glenda bustled about the room, clearing the breakfast things away and saying how amazing it would be to have a little girl like Isabella around all the time.

The two babies fell asleep after their milk and Isabella realised it was time to go. She had completely lost track of time. Hoping her mother wouldn't be angry with her, she hugged her new friends goodbye.

"Wait," said Gaffey and he popped a little ruby gem in the palm of her hand. "This is for you to remember us by."

She thanked him and stooped to get through the door without banging her head.

Soon she was skipping down the hill again.

"Ouch!"

"Ay up!"

"Eek!"

"Ooh!"

And she was down the silly steps. Then along the path, through the cave the other way, and out of Gnomeland altogether.

She looked around for the ginger castle cat, but it was nowhere to be seen. She quickened her step, worrying that she'd be late, and ran all the way back to the big park gate.

She slowed down to listen as she passed the courtyard and the swimming pool and stood on her tiptoes to peer through the window again.

There was James, still splashing away, and Auntie Alison and Mum chatting together on sun loungers. They hadn't even noticed she'd gone! And looking down at her own feet, she noticed the ginger cat had joined her again, purring and circling her ankles as if delighted to see her.

Later, when she told the others where she'd been, it seemed no one believed her. Mum said she did, but raised her eyebrows and said something about her having a wonderful imagination. However, when the park had opened and they were all in Gnomeland together, Isabella took James to see Gaffey and Glenda's house.

"I went through there," she said, pointing at the little door and not expecting him to take her seriously.

James stepped into the little gravel garden and knocked at the door. There was, of course, no answer. He tried to open it, but it wouldn't budge. She waited for him to say something cruel or accuse her of fibbing. She felt silly and began to wonder if it had all been a dream…

…but just then she felt something small and hard in the pocket of her cat dress.

The ruby gem!

It hadn't been a dream. She hadn't imagined it after all. It had really happened!

She showed it to James.

He looked at her, his eyes glowing with excitement, and said:

"Take me on your next adventure, Isabella!"

The End